our
generation®

This is Willow's story.

WILLOW™

THE MOST FANTABULOUS PAJAMA PARTY EVER

BY

SUSAN CAPPADONIA LOVE

ILLUSTRATED BY TRISH ROUELLE

An Our Generation® *book*

MAISON JOSEPH BATTAT LTD. *Publisher*

A very special thanks to the editor,
Joanne Burke Casey.

Our Generation® Books is a registered trademark of Maison Joseph Battat Ltd.
Text copyright © 2012 by Susan Love
ISBN: 978-0-9844904-7-9
Printed in China

For Hannah and
her big sis, Emma.

Read all the adventures in the
Our Generation® Book Series

One Smart Cookie
featuring Hally™

Blizzard on Moose Mountain
featuring Katelyn™

Stars in Your Eyes
featuring Sydney Lee™

The Note in the Piano
featuring Mary Lyn™

The Mystery of the Vanishing Coin
featuring Eva®

Adventures at Shelby Stables
featuring Lily Anna®

The Sweet Shoppe Mystery
featuring Jenny™

The Jumpstart Squad
featuring Juliet™

The Dress in the Window
featuring Audrey-Ann®

The Jukebox Babysitters
featuring Ashley-Rose™

In the Limelight
featuring Evelyn™

The Most Fantabulous Pajama Party Ever
featuring Willow™

Read more about **Our Generation®** books and dolls online:
www.ogdolls.com

CONTENTS

EXTRA! EXTRA! READ ALL ABOUT IT!
*Big words, wacky words, powerful words, funny words...
what do they all mean? They are marked with this symbol *.
Look them up in the Glossary at the end of this book.*

Chapter One

WHERE AM I?

"Look at that whopper of a bump on her forehead!" my classmate, Sawyer, squealed. "It's turning purple! Yikes!"

"Are you okay, Willow?" cried Daisy, one of my best friends.

"Someone call 911!" barked my teacher, Mr. Floof, who is known to exaggerate*.

I squinted at the crowd of faces staring down at me. They all looked worried, except for Sawyer, who seemed amazed.

Squeezing my eyes shut, I tried to turn my head away from them. Ow!

If I were a cartoon character, there would be a tiny tornado swirling over my head to show how dizzy I felt, and stars bursting all around it.

In real life, there were no stars and no tiny, swirling tornado. There was, however, Sawyer's pointer finger, which he waggled* wildly near my injury.

His finger was covered in powdery, bright orange crumbs. With each jab in the air, I got a strong whiff of the puffed cheesy curls that he packs every day for his snack.

I felt sick.

The same smelly stuff was crusted around Sawyer's mouth, too, looking like lipstick gone wrong.

I wanted to get up, but just couldn't make myself budge.

It was like hoping to sail a sailboat on a windless day. Or stepping into deep snow and trying to run. Or riding a bicycle when the chain falls off.

In other words, impossible!

What's going on here? I wondered. *Where am I?*

V-e-r-y s-l-o-w-l-y my brain began working. It was Monday morning. I'd been jumping rope in the school gym. Daisy and I were partners, as we always are.

The tip of my sneaker had gotten caught on the rope. I'd tripped and smacked my forehead on the edge of a folding table. WHAPP! Then I'd fallen backwards. BAMM!

Oh, the embarrassment*!

Usually I am one of the best jump ropers in my class. This morning though, when we'd decided to try double Dutch*, I'd felt tired and clumsy and blue*. *But why?* I wondered.

Dizziness began mixing with dread*. Something crept into my mind. That something was what had happened the day before.

That something was my dream of having the most fantabulous* birthday pajama party ever—destroyed!

Chapter Two

DOWN THE DRAIN

I'd had my 10th birthday party planned for a long, long time. It was finally going to happen in just one month. Or so I thought.

The invitations I'd made for my five best friends announced:

I could just picture Anny, Abrianna, Sadie, Daisy, Charlotte (whose nickname is Charlie) and me having a fantabulous time, playing fantabulous party games and giving each other fantabulous new hairstyles.

We'd dress-up our dolls, eat birthday cake and play flashlight tag. Then we'd put our PJs on and giggle in our sleeping bags until we fell asleep (which would be *way* past our usual bedtimes).

Sometimes I felt like I'd burst if I had to wait another moment for my birthday to arrive. But now, still in a heap on the gym floor, all I could focus on was the day before. Sunday was when my fantabulous plans went downhill, fast.

Sunday's (Turn of) Events

1:10 p.m.   Feeling fine! Humming and singing as I got ready to go to Beth Ann's Backyard Birthday Bash*. Beth Ann is on my swim team. I thought it was really nice that she was having a little cookout for her birthday.

1:52 p.m.   Positively bursting with happiness! On our way to Beth Ann's, my dad stopped at a post office mailbox. I dropped five bright green envelopes with glittering purple polka dots into the mailbox. Invitations to my most fantabulous birthday party ever were on their way.

1:59 p.m.   Still overflowing with excitement! As I skipped up Beth Ann's driveway I spotted my BFFs* and thought about how thrilled they would be when they opened their invitations.

2:02 p.m.   Mood fizzling*. All it took was one look at Beth Ann's so-called backyard (which, as it turns out, is as big as a football field). There was a mammoth* inflatable* water slide, bumper cars, a zip line and cotton candy machine. Not a little cookout. Oh-no. It was more like a huge carnival. This was a disastrophe! (That's my own made-up word that combines the word disaster with catastrophe, which means it's even worse than terrible!)

2:16 p.m. Nearly fainted. Anny, Sadie, Daisy, Abrianna, Charlie and I saw some scruffy-looking guys setting up guitars, a drum set and microphones on a large stage. Sadie asked who was performing and a guy told us it was the enormously popular teen band called Purple Seven! I have a poster of them hanging above my bed.

2:17 p.m. Sadness set in as I thought to myself: *How could I have the most fantabulous birthday party ever when I was already at the most fantabulous birthday party ever?*

2:19 p.m. Up for the challenge. I decide to figure out a new plan for making my party extra-super-duper-fantabulous. *But I'll think about it later*, I said to myself. Beth Ann's party rocked, so why waste a great party on a bad mood?

Those memories came rushing back to me as Mr. Floof helped me to my feet. I was wobbly, but feeling better.

Sawyer shouted out one of his annoying riddles, "Hey Willow, what's the hardest thing about learning how to do double Dutch?"

Before anyone could answer, he boomed, "The FLOOR!"

This was followed by bursts of laughter.

Mr. Floof held my arm steady and led me to the nurse's office, where I flopped down on a creaky blue plastic chair. The nurse gave me a squishy ice pack and told me to hold it on my forehead for five minutes.

My bright red watch read 10:26. The teeny-tiny dog bone on the end of the second hand circled around and around the puppy in the center.

Big sigh.

I had to admit that Beth Ann's party was a blast. That's what all my classmates, Beth Ann's gymnastic class, our swim team, her soccer buddies and about 100 other party guests thought, too.

It was completely over the top*!

One thing was for sure: my party would wow none of my friends now that they'd been at Beth Ann's marvelous, incredible, gigantic party.

What can I do to live up to what I've

written on my invitations? I worried. *How can I make my party the most fantabulous birthday party ever?*

There was only one thing to do and that was rethink my plans.

My forehead and hand were getting numb from the ice pack. I checked my watch. It said 10:28. Three more minutes.

The nurse let me use a sheet of plain paper and a pencil. I started writing a new invitation using my free hand. The letters were somewhat shaky looking, but it was readable.

By the time five minutes were up, my new and improved party was planned from beginning to end. I must say, it really was fantabulous.

Now all I had to do was convince my mom that it could be sensational.

কৈ কৈ

It's never easy to deliver bad news.

My babysitter, Matisse, tried the best she

18

could a few days later. "I'm sorry, Willow, but you have to finish your Spanish and math homework before you can go outside and play."

"But the Dooleys are challenging the Tuckers in softball in a few minutes!" I protested.

I live on Dooley Drive. The next street over is Tucker Lane. Even though the streets are side by side, and our backyards even touch, Dooley Drive and Tucker Lane are actually in two different towns.

The kids that live on these streets go to two different schools and we nicknamed ourselves after the streets we live on.

We're friends, but we're always trying to outdo each other. It's the Dooleys against the Tuckers in kickball. In softball. In tag. In just about everything.

Matisse continued, "Your friends might have to do without you today. Unless, of course, you get moving and finish this homework ASAP*."

For a college kid, Matisse sure is strict sometimes, which is just about every day after school until my mom gets home from work.

While sports come easily to me, school doesn't. I would always rather be outside playing than sitting at the kitchen table doing homework with Matisse.

If you ask me, the only good things about homework are my two kittens, Puff and Priscilla, who snuggle up on my lap and purr while I practice Spanish flashcards.

"Okay, okay," I huffed, "but I won't ever need to know any of this Spanish and math stuff anyway!"

"That's not true," Matisse pointed out. "Without math, you'd never know when it was time to celebrate being one billion seconds old."

"Whaaaaat?" I said with half of a smile. Matisse tries to trick me into having fun with math. She sneaks in wacky stuff like this a lot.

For example, Matisse gives my mom math brainteasers to tuck into my lunch bag. My mom said I'm special because I'm the one and only member of Matisse's Lunch Box Riddle Club.

"Think about it," Matisse said excitedly. "Turning one billion seconds old is a big moment in your life. You don't want to miss a huge birthday celebration like that!"

I got out my calculator and she showed me how to do the math. We discovered that I will be one billion *seconds* old when I am almost 32 years old (to be specific, when I'm 31 years old plus 251 days).

"Good job, Willow," Matisse praised. "Now let's figure something else out. But you won't need a calculator for this problem."

I groaned. "What are we figuring out now?"

"The reason why you're grumpy today," Matisse replied.

"No reason," I mumbled*, rubbing a big pink eraser angrily across a doodle in my notebook.

"C'mon, what's up?" she asked softly.

I took a deep breath. "Now that Anny, Sadie, Abrianna and Charlie have been to Beth Ann's fancy party, they don't seem all that excited to come to mine."

Matisse put her arm around my shoulders. "I'm sure that's not true, Willow."

With the strength of a super-hero, I continued making messy, dark eraser smudges on the lined paper. "To make matters worse,

Daisy did not even mention that she got my invitation."

Matisse frowned. "They're your best friends. They absolutely want to be at your birthday party."

What she said made perfect sense IF you weren't there to see Anny, Sadie, Abrianna and Charlie behaving strangely when I asked if they were coming to my party.

They looked down, and away, and not into my eyes. They shuffled their feet around and seemed awkward*.

They are *my best friends*, I thought, *so why were they acting weird?*

Chapter Three

SCHOOL PRIDE

As soon as I finished my homework, Matisse and I raced out the door and ran to the sports field that was on Tucker Lane. The game was tied.

The Dooleys (Lucia, JJ, Luke, Syd, Rio, Haley and Ayla) were psyched to see me. I got up to bat and hit a home run. The Dooleys won!

On our walk home from the game, Matisse and I saw my neighbor, Captain Cabot, in his garden. He earned his nickname because he had been a sea captain for many years.

Captain Cabot was trying to "encourage" his dog, Pirate, to come to him by bribing him with a dog treat. Pirate already had something tasty in his mouth, though. It looked very much like one of my cowboy boots I'd left on the back porch.

Pirate is a lovable Dalmatian who's also a real mischief-maker. He's constantly escaping from the house and frolicking* around the neighborhood. His main goal is to steal kids' flip-flops, softball mitts and basically anything he can get his paws on. Then he buries those objects in Captain Cabot's garden.

With Pirate finally safe on his leash, Captain Cabot asked me how everything was going.

"Great!" I said. "Except there's too much homework."

"Be happy you have a school to go to," Captain Cabot said, as he pulled a small picture out of his wallet. He tapped the photo, which showed two teenagers standing in front of a simple brick building.

Matisse and I leaned in to get a good look at the picture while Captain Cabot told us an interesting story.

"Those are my grandkids in Kenya," he said proudly. "They went there with a group called Free The Children and helped build this school because the village didn't have one."

Imagine not having a school to go to, I thought. My life would be so different.

I wouldn't be able to be in the school play or go on field trips. I wouldn't be able to win special prizes for perfect penmanship or help plant the school garden.

If I couldn't read and write, how could I be a scientist like my mom? Or get a license to be a bus driver like my dad?

రావ రావ

That night I was extra helpful before dinner rolled around. I volunteered to set the table before my mom asked me to. I went to the garden to pick basil leaves for the spaghetti sauce. I washed lettuce and grated carrots for our tossed salad.

"Ohhhhhhh Mom-mi-o," I said in a singsong voice. "I want to ask you a favor."

She raised her eyebrows. "I had a feeling you might."

I explained that my friends probably thought my party sounded pretty boring compared to Beth Ann's party.

Then, in my this-is-no-big-deal tone of voice, I suggested that maybe, just maybe, we needed to make a few tweaks* to the party plans.

"Willow, don't worry," my mom said. "Your party is going to be wonderful. Your friends will love it because you planned all the activities around their favorite things to do."

She had a good point.

Anny loves doing hair, so I had made a big poster that read:

Anny's Salon
Featuring 22 Stylish & Silly Hairstyles

I'd cut out pictures of hairstyles from magazines and glued them on the poster, with the style name under each picture.

There were pigtails, side ponies, side-swept styles, twisty buns, French braids, mini braids and curls galore*. We would practice the hairstyles on each other and take our photos. Everything we'd need was in my dress-up trunk, ready for glamour.

Especially for Sadie and Abrianna (who are both big-time game lovers), I'd invented two new games for us to play that were giggle-arious (my own made-up word combining giggle and hilarious*).

Charlie is a chocoholic, so I'd picked chocolate as the flavor for my birthday cake, with pink and orange frosting and chocolate ice cream. Because Daisy is an outdoor adventurer, we'd play flashlight tag in the dark in my yard.

It's true that these are our favorite things to do together, I thought, *but I want this party to be super special. Amazing. Sensational. Fantabulous!*

"Pleeeeeeeeeeeease, Mom," I begged. "Can you pleeeeeeease just take a peek at my even-better ideas?"

I handed her the new and improved invitation I'd made in the nurse's office. I was bouncing up and down with excitement.

As she read it, the invitation started shaking in her hand. I glanced* up at her face and saw she was holding in a silent laugh as she read.

She covered her mouth with her hand to hide her smile. "A chocolate fountain?! Bungee jumping?!"

"Doesn't that sound like fun?" I asked hopefully.

"Blimp rides?!" she hooted.

"You know, those huge puffy airships that float across the sky," I explained. "The ones that kind of look like gigantic jelly bean–shaped balloons with fins?"

My mom nodded. "Yes, Willow, I know exactly what you're talking about."

"Wouldn't that be incredible?!" I exclaimed.

"That *certainly* would be." My mom chuckled* while shaking her head no no no.

It looked like my new and improved invitation was going to be sent Express Delivery—to the trashcan, that is.

Chapter Four

FINALLY!

Thunder boomed across the night sky. Rain pounded on our roof. Wind rattled the windows. Priscilla and Puff didn't mind a bit. They were curled up at the end of my bed.

I adjusted my birdie pillow just so under my head, pulled my cozy blanket all the way up to my chin, and worried. In addition to my party problem, something else had been troubling me. I'd been thinking about what Captain Cabot had told me.

Earlier that night, my mom and I had gone on the Internet together to find out more about Free The Children.

"Listen to this," I read from the website, "Free The Children was started in 1995 by a 12-year-old boy. Now they've built more than

650 schools around the world."

My mom pointed at the screen. "It says here that out of the world's 130 million children not able to go to school, 70% are girls."

"That's unfair! Why?" I clicked on a button and read the explanation.

Many of the kids have to work to support their families. Often there's no school available. And even if there is a school, in some places it's the girls' job to collect water for their families to survive. They might have to walk for hours each day to get to a river and carry the water home. That forces them to miss school.

Sadly, as unfair as it may seem, girls miss the chance for their own education so their brothers can go to school. In many parts of the world, girls don't have the same importance as boys.

However, Free The Children found a solution to the problem. They built schools with wells, so the students could carry fresh, clean water home with them. Other schools were built with rooftops that allow rain to drain into big containers, making the water safe for drinking. That way girls could go to school *and* bring water home with them.

We looked at pictures on the website of kids in China, Kenya, India, Ecuador and Haiti. Some showed kids who were proudly smiling and studying in their new schools. They looked a lot like my own friends and me.

There were also photos of the kids in the USA and Canada who had raised money to help pay for the schools. They held bake sales, penny drives, walkathons, you name it.

"Wow! Did you know that kids raise most of Free The Children's funds* so schools can be built?" I asked.

❧ ❧

That thought was still in my head as I fell asleep that night. When I woke up the next morning, I knew exactly what I was going to do.

I'd have the most fantabulous lemonade stand ever to help raise money for a new school.

There was much to do and I knew just where to turn for help. To my neighborhood friends, the Dooleys.

On my way to the school cafeteria a few days later, I peeked into my lunch bag. A piece of lined yellow paper was tucked inside:

<u>More calculator fun</u>
<u>from the Lunch Box Riddle Club</u>
What does Pirate steal
and plant in Captain Cabot's garden?
(Hint: They come in many sizes,
but are still always one foot long!)
To find the answer, do this math on your calculator.
10609 × 5 =
Now turn your calculator upside down!

Pulling my calculator out of my backpack, I punched in the numbers. The answer, spelled out in upside-down numbers, made me giggle out loud. Ha!

I headed to my lunch table with Matisse's yellow paper in my hand. Her brainteasers had become a craze* at my school. Everyone wanted to try them, including my friends. But today my besties* were already excitedly talking.

Sadie saw me coming. "Willow, your party sounds awesome!"

Wahoo! Finally some enthusiasm! I thought.

"I can definitely come," Charlie chimed in.

"Charlie means she can definitely come and gobble up the chocolate fountain," joked Abrianna.

Uh-ohhhhhhh, I thought. *This isn't right.*

"Do you think we'll be able to see our houses from up in the blimp?" Anny asked hopefully.

"I've always wanted to bungee jump!" said Abrianna.

Double uh-oh!

Anny looked guilty. "Sorry I spilled the

beans*, Willow. My mom and I stopped by last night to lend a book to your mom. You were at swim practice. Anyway, I read the new invitation you made that was sitting on the kitchen counter—"

Daisy cut her off. "You're going to mail the invitations to *all* of us, right?"

There were two reasons why Daisy's comment surprised me. One, she hadn't really spoken too much to me the last couple of days. I thought she was mad at me for some reason, but I couldn't figure out what it was. And Two, she sounded like she was blaming me for something. Strange.

"Of course—no wait! What I mean is—" The shrill* school bell drowned out my voice and everyone scrambled off to brush their hair. It was school picture day, and our class was being photographed right after lunch.

There wasn't another word about my party. I couldn't decide if that was a good thing or not.

Chapter Five

AN EARLY SURPRISE

The Tuckers crushed the Dooleys in touch football after school. As we walked back to our street with Matisse, I pitched my idea to the Dooleys about raising money to help build a school.

First they joked about how lucky some kids are to not have to go to school. But the more I explained about what I'd seen on the website, the more questions they had.

I told them about the schools that are built to allow children to carry water home with them.

Syd sounded confused. "I don't get it. What's the big deal about water?"

"Good question," I answered. "Many of these kids' homes aren't like ours. They don't have water that comes out of a faucet."

The Dooleys' mouths dropped open. It was hard to believe that you'd have to walk miles to get water to cook, bathe or hand-wash clothes—or to drink!

Because there's no running water or bathrooms or kitchens or refrigerators, entire families survive on buckets of water that girls carry. Girls have a better chance of being able to go to school if they can bring water home with them.

"We could help kids thousands of miles away," I said. "With new schools, they will learn how to read, do math and run their own businesses some day. That means they could have better, healthier, less poor futures."

Everyone nodded their heads. Ours would be the most fantabulous lemonade stand ever. To seal the deal, we each put our left foot forward and began the Dooley cheer (stomp-stomp, clap-clap, left elbow in the air, right-leg karate kick, jump high, slap hands, yee-hah!).

Since we still had an hour before dinnertime, we decided to get going. The very first stand would open in three days.

The Dooleys sprawled* out under a shady tree in my yard. Matisse helped us make a list of items we'd need, speaking mostly in Spanish so we could practice our vocabulary*.

"*Para el Sábado* (For Saturday)," she said, "*necesitan limónes, azúcar, tazas y hielo* (you will need lemons, sugar, cups and ice). "What else?"

I scribbled the words in my notebook as items were added.

"*Papel y crayónes* (paper and crayons) to make posters," shouted Lucia.

"*Una mesa* (a table) for the stand," Syd added.

"*Sillas* (chairs)," called out JJ.

When the list of supplies was complete, the Dooleys made another list of things that needed to be done and who wanted to do what. We'd start the following day after school.

After my homework was done the next day, the Dooleys regrouped in my yard. Syd, Rio and Luke put the lemonade stand together with the help of Matisse and Captain Cabot. Lucia and I fetched tape and scissors.

Captain Cabot used wood to build the frame for an awning.

Matisse fished a tape measure out of her extra-large purse and handed it to me.

Syd and I measured the table, which helped us figure out how long to make the streamer of colorful triangle-shaped flags. It would decorate the front of the stand.

Haley and Ayla drew thick, bold arrows on paper signs. We'd hang those by the Tucker Sports Field on Saturday morning to direct people to our street.

I'd printed out facts from the Free The Children website, and Haley and Ayla copied them onto a big poster board. Pirate liked the poster so much he snatched it and trotted off lickety-split before we could catch him.

He'd escaped from the house again and we knew where he was headed. Rio, Matisse and I ran to Captain Cabot's flower garden. Sure enough, Pirate was madly digging a hole to bury the poster in.

Matisse always keeps a doggy treat in her purse. Pirate's ears perked up as soon as he smelled it and he leaped over to Matisse.

"Good boy, Pirate," she said, giving him

the treat and taking hold of his collar at the same time.

He wagged his tail and licked his chops*, forgetting all about burying the poster.

Captain Cabot came out of the shed where he spends most of his day tinkering*. He was carrying a large, beat-up cardboard box. He took one look at the teeth marks and drool on the poster and shook his head.

"Pirate is half robber and half magician," he said. "Never been able to figure out how he gets out of the house! Tell the Dooleys I'm sorry about that poster."

Captain Cabot held the box out to me. "This gift is for you, Willow. I know your birthday isn't for two-and-a-half weeks, but it will come in handy now."

"Oh goody! Thank you!" I was sure it was one of Captain Cabot's off-the-wall* inventions.

Perhaps he was giving me the toaster he invented that glows in the dark (perfect for midnight snackers).

Maybe the gift was the tennis racket that congratulates you when you hit the ball (what a great confidence builder).

Or the bike that plays music when you pedal (so you can hum while you ride).

A wide strip of clear tape sealed the box flaps closed. I peeled it off and found wadded up balls of old newspaper inside.

Trying not to crinkle my nose at the musty* smell, I dug around until my fingertips touched a smooth metal object.

I was speechless.

What do you say about a big, old brass bell? It was dark brown and tarnished* with a green coating on it here and there.

I held it up.

"It's very...heavy!" I exclaimed, then instantly felt foolish.

Captain Cabot had a good belly laugh about that.

The bell was about six inches high, with a loop handle on the top. I swung the braided rope on the bottom back and forth and gave it a good ring.

"It has a really nice sound!" I said, this time meaning it.

"There's a story behind this bell," Captain Cabot told me. "This is no ordinary bell. It's lucky. Really really lucky!"

"It's lucky?" That sounded interesting.

"You bet," he replied. "This bell was on

my ship. Every time we set out to sea in fog we rang it so other boats would know we were close by." As Captain Cabot remembered the story, his face was happy and his eyes seemed a little watery.

"It always brought us home safely, even during the thickest fog I've seen in my entire life as a sea captain." He pointed to the bell. "It will bring good luck to your lemonade stand, too."

"Hello there!" greeted my mom. She had just gotten home from work and was walking up our driveway carrying grocery bags. She looked pretty in the sparkly beaded necklace I made her for Valentine's Day last year.

"Look what Captain Cabot gave me, Mom. It's an early birthday present!"

"If the Dooleys ring it every time a cup of lemonade is sold, it will bring more good luck!" Captain Cabot promised.

"Then we will," I said. "Thank you so much."

We said goodbye to Captain Cabot and Pirate, and then to Matisse, who was going back to her college dorm* to study.

As I helped put away the groceries, I told my mom about the lemonade stand.

She gave me a quick kiss on the top of my head. "I'm so proud of you for deciding to help other kids. And I'm proud you're getting the Dooleys organized, too."

That made me feel great. And since my mom was in such a good mood, it seemed like perfect timing to bring up my new party idea.

I'd never had a chance to tell my friends the truth about the mix-up with the invitation. They still believed that there would be a chocolate fountain, bungee jumping and blimp rides at my party.

It was going to be hugely disappointing when they found out that none of those things would happen.

*If only the party could be bigger, better, grander**, I thought. *If only Mom says yes.*

"Ohhhhhhhh Mom-mi-o," I said a bit too brightly. "I was thinking...."

"Oh boy," she teased, "I saw this coming."

"It's nothing much," I said, "it's just that I was thinking maybe we could invite all the girls in my class to the party. You know, make it bigger."

She stopped unloading the dishwasher and looked directly in my eyes. "I wish we could, honey, I really do. But we simply don't have room for 19 sleepover guests."

"But wouldn't it be so much fun?" I pleaded. "Beth Ann had a gazillion guests, and it was such a blast!"

"Her celebration wasn't a sleepover. And your party WILL be fun," she said, "because you'll be with your five best friends."

"Does that mean no?" I pouted.

"I'm afraid so," she admitted.

This party is turning out to be floperrible, I thought. (That's my own made-up word combining flop and terrible, meaning a total failure and awful.) My friends had seemed so fired up. How could I possibly break the news to them?

Chapter Six

WORKS LIKE MAGIC

Matisse bargained with me the next day. "After you're done with your Spanish homework, we'll walk to the corner market to get lemonade stand supplies."

"Deal," I said, then remembered I didn't have any cash.

"I'll lend it to you, and you can pay me back after you make gobs of money at the stand on Saturday," she said.

"Why is this homework taking soooooooooo long?" I complained.

"Because it takes twice as long to learn Spanish when you're sulking* about your party," she said.

"Okay, okay," I grumbled. Another day had gone by and I still hadn't fessed up to my friends that the invitation wasn't real.

51

Finally, I finished my Spanish homework and off we went to the store.

While I collected the items on the list, Matisse struck* up a conversation in Spanish with the owner, a woman named Señora Sanchez.

They were talking fast, but I understood a few words. Matisse said something about *una chica* (a young girl). And Señora Sanchez replied, "*Está muy nerviosa* (She's very nervous)."

Were they talking about me? I worried. *Were they disgusted at how I sort of let my best friends believe the fake party plans?*

The grand opening of our first lemonade stand was Saturday morning in front of my house.

We squeezed fresh lemons and mixed the juice in pitchers with water and sugar.

Except for Haley and Ayla, who had piano lessons that morning, the Dooleys were all there, ready for thirsty customers.

Priscilla was there, too. JJ and I took turns holding and petting her. Puff was inside the house, snoozing in a ray of sunshine streaming through the window.

Sawyer was our first customer. He'd just played in a soccer game and had seen the signs we'd hung near the exit of the Tucker Sports Field.

Gulping down his cupful in one swallow, Sawyer burped loudly and said, "Hey, Willow, here's a good one. What do you get if you let your cat drink lemonade?"

As usual, before anyone could make a guess, he blurted out, "A SOURpuss!" He elbowed Luke. "Like lemons are sour? And a cat is called a puss? A SOURpuss!"

A few of the other customers in line laughed, but not as much as Sawyer did.

Lots of soccer, softball and basketball players, coaches and parents bought lemonade. Matisse and her roommate came, too.

All of our customers said it was the most

delicious, ice-cold lemonade they'd ever tasted. Not too sweet and not too tart*.

So many people came, the Dooleys were ringing the bell like crazy!

Every time we rang the bell, Pirate howled with joy.

That's why our neighbor, Mr. Hissanfuss, called my mom to complain about all the noise. "They woke up my baby who was taking a nap! Now she's howling louder than Pirate!"

Two of the Tuckers pedaled by the lemonade stand on their bikes. One of them sped off down the street. The other one, wearing a zebra-striped helmet and a matching zebra-striped backpack, slowed down and scowled*, but didn't buy any lemonade.

That's odd, I thought.

ৎঌ ঌৎ

A few minutes after noon, the most fantabulous lemonade stand ever closed because we ran out of lemonade. Every last drop had been sold.

"Captain Cabot was right," I exclaimed, "the lucky bell really IS lucky!"

"We made a fortune!" announced Rio.

Once we payed Matisse back for the lemonade supplies, we counted the money.

We were shocked. There was very little left to donate to the new school. If it hadn't been for the nice dad who gave us an extra $10 for the school fund, we wouldn't have made any money at all.

"I have an idea," I said. "What if we ask people to donate the supplies? Then all the cash will go into the school fund."

"My aunt owns a party supply store," said Lucia. "I can ask if she'll donate cups."

"My cousin, Jenny, runs a small bakery business and might be willing to give us sugar," suggested Haley.

"We could all make ice and bring it for tomorrow," said JJ. "That would also save money."

56

Syd added, "And I'll ask my parents if I can bring the napkins that are left over from our family picnic."

"Señora Sanchez at the corner market might donate the lemons," I said.

Matisse nodded. "Good idea, Willow. It will be great practice to speak in Spanish with Señora Sanchez when you ask her."

I must have looked at Matisse as if she had three heads with unicorn horns, because she laughed and said, "Trust me. You can do it, Willow."

"How about if we ask my mom if she'll donate lemons instead?" I asked.

"C'mon, Willow," Matisse encouraged, "let's try a pretend conversation in Spanish. I'll be Señora Sanchez and you can be you."

We practiced what I'd say over and over in Spanish until I didn't stumble over my words. Then we practiced some more as we walked to the corner market.

"*¡Hola! Buenas tardes* (Hi! Good afternoon), Señora Sanchez," I began nervously when we entered the store. Even though I had to speak slowly and needed a tiny bit of help from Matisse, the conversation went smoothly.

Señora Sanchez was impressed that I'd learned how to ask for a donation in her language. She also liked the fact that the Dooleys were doing something to make a difference in the world.

"*Estoy feliz dandote límones* (I'm happy

to give you lemons)," she said with a big smile.

"*Muchas gracias* (Thank you so much)," I told her.

It was a good thing Lucia, JJ and Luke came with us to the market, because we walked home with five crates of juicy lemons.

చ౨ ౬చ

"You're getting that lucky bell nice and shiny for the lemonade stand tomorrow morning," said my mom.

I continued rubbing it with a soft cloth that Captain Cabot had given to me. The blacker that the cloth got, the shinier the bell became.

To be truthful, the real reason I was polishing the bell was because I was hoping its good luck would rub off on me. I needed it!

The kids at school were still talking about Beth Ann's over-the-top party.

"Off the charts," raved one classmate.

"The party to beat all other parties," a

girl on my swim team said.

Most people (including me) could describe it in one word: amazing.

It wasn't that I wanted to compete with Beth Ann. I really didn't. I just wanted my party to be a ton of fun, too.

How could my friends not compare her party with mine? They were just one month apart. And they were both birthday parties.

Daisy still hadn't told me if she could come to my party. I was afraid to ask because I was scared to hear that her answer might be "No."

I put all of my attention into shining the bell, getting in every crack until it gleamed.

Holding the bell inches from my face, I whispered, "You brought luck to the lemonade stand. Now if you can only work your magic on me."

The Dooleys started their second day in the lemonade stand business with so many customers that we ran out of lemonade again.

Thanks to Señora Sanchez, there was plenty of fruit to make more. We all dashed inside the house to bring out another crate of lemons, get the bag of sugar and refill three pitchers with water.

When we returned to the stand, we saw what looked like a few soccer players headed toward us.

Haley and Ayla quickly squeezed the lemons, Rio measured the sugar and Lucia and JJ stirred the contents of the pitchers with large wooden spoons.

After the first soccer player paid for his lemonade, I reached over to grab the rope handle of the bell. But the rope handle wasn't there—and neither was the bell!

Chapter Seven

THOSE COPYCATS!

Had the bell fallen off the table? Not that we could see. Had someone brought it inside and set it down? Nope. It was nowhere to be found.

That lucky bell had brought a lot of business twice in a row. We were counting on it to bring even more for the school fund.

"Things don't just disappear," said JJ.

"They do if they're stolen," replied Lucia.

"By those Tuckers," Rio spat out.

"They'd definitely pull something like that," said Ayla. "They're always trying to be better than us."

"You saw how they were spying on us," Haley accused.

"Biking down our street doesn't mean

they were spying," Luke objected.

"We don't have proof that they took the bell," Syd said. "We can't accuse them."

"Maybe Mr. Hissanfuss took it," said Haley.

Luke agreed. "You might be right. It's almost his baby's naptime."

"It seems like Mr. Hissanfuss would call my mom before he did something like that," I said.

"Maybe not," said JJ. "He was pretty upset that we woke up his baby."

"How can we explain this to Captain Cabot?" I asked.

"Well...what if it was Captain Cabot who kind of borrowed it?" Rio asked.

"What?" I said. "No way!"

"No, I mean maybe he missed it and will return it later," Rio said. "You saw how he got misty-eyed when he gave it to you."

We had a lot of time to discuss it. Business was slow for the rest of the day even though there were games at the Tucker Sports Field until 3:00 p.m.

There was only one explanation why sales had dropped off suddenly.

Our lemonade business had gone sour without the lucky bell.

Discouraged and angry, we began to take down the signs and put away the chairs, napkins and cups.

Luke called out to a boy he knew who was passing by with his dad. "Hey, Landis! Come and get some ice-cold lemonade!"

"Sorry kids, we already bought lemonade from a stand around the corner," said the dad.

"Okay, maybe next time," I said, trying to be polite. "By the way, where is the other stand?"

"Right across from the sports field," said Landis.

"On Tucker Lane," added the dad, as they continued on their way.

Those Tuckers! Those copycats! First they

stole our bell, and then they stole our business!

While we cleaned up, we grumbled to one another about the nerve of the Tuckers.

"I'll freeze these two-and-a-half pitchers of lemonade that are left," Haley suggested. "We can thaw them out and use them next weekend."

"What's the use?" Lucia said. "We'll just sit at the stand twiddling our thumbs while the Tuckers get all the customers from the sports field."

"Giving up on the lemonade stand would mean giving up our dream to help build a school," Luke said.

"We made a promise to help kids," Rio reminded us.

"And we made a promise to ourselves," Syd added.

"Let's step up our business," I said. "Offer something different from what the Tuckers are selling at their stand."

"How about selling cupcakes?" said

Haley. "My cousin, Jenny, the one with the baking business, is sleeping over next weekend. We'll make some of her famous cupcakes to sell at the stand."

"I can play the flute," said JJ. "That might attract customers."

We did the Dooley cheer (left foot forward, stomp-stomp, clap-clap, left elbow in the air, right-leg karate kick, jump high, slap hands, yee-hah!). Now that we had a new plan, our mood was greatly improved.

Daisy's mood, however, continued to be unfriendly toward me. When she chose someone else as her partner for double Dutch jump roping a few days later at recess, my feelings were truly hurt.

What's her problem? I wondered.

While we waited for our turns to jump rope, Abrianna, Sadie, Charlie and Anny stood and chatted. All they talked about was the blimp ride, which made me fidgety* and nervous.

I couldn't get up the courage I needed to tell them the truth. It was too hard because I'd let the fib* go on for so long.

My party was getting closer. And I was getting more anxious*.

❧ ❧

The Dooleys were all geared up on the following Saturday to have the neighborhood's finest, most fantabulous lemonade stand ever. We thawed the lemonade from the weekend before, then squeezed more fresh lemons in case we ran out.

JJ brought her flute to draw a crowd to the stand. Haley's cousin, Jenny, brought her famous "Blue Zinger" cupcakes to sell. They were blue all over, with blue icing, blue sugar sprinkles and blue paper wrappers. They were delicious (I bought two!).

Señora Sanchez stopped by with a girl who looked like she was about my age. She introduced the girl as her niece, Alejandra, who was visiting from Peru. (I knew from Spanish lessons that the "H" sound in her name is actually a "J".)

We told Señora Sanchez they didn't have to pay because she had donated the lemons, but she insisted.

Alejandra was shy and nervous. I got up my courage to talk to her in Spanish. We were able to speak a few sentences back and forth. Matisse would have been so proud of me.

After they left, we heard a noise that sounded like an angry elephant. JJ stopped playing the flute and we all listened.

"Is that a tuba I hear?" asked Lucia. "Is that sound coming from Tucker Lane?"

"Interesting," said Ayla. "I've never heard any of the Tuckers playing a tuba before."

Seconds later, a bunch of guys in long basketball shorts and matching sleeveless shirts came around the corner toward the Dooleys. One of them was dribbling a ball and the rest were eating, drinking and joking around as they walked.

"Do you mind if I put this in your trash can?" one of the guys asked, as the group got close to us. He took the final swig from a white paper cup and crumpled it up. Then he pretended the cup was a basketball that he was shooting into a hoop.

Another kid tossed an empty purple cupcake wrapper in our trash. "Geez, what are the chances of having two lemonade stands one street apart?" he said.

"Yeah," his friend replied, "especially

two stands that both sell cupcakes and both have musicians, too."

Grrrrrrrrrrr! Those Tuckers were copying us again!

Chapter Eight

SPIES AMONG US

"If the Tuckers open a stand today, they might have lemonade and cupcakes," Lucia fumed* on Sunday, "but they won't have popcorn or painted rocks like us."

"And they won't have a dancing yellow chicken," Rio said through an enormous beak. He was wearing last year's Halloween costume to draw attention to our stand.

Sawyer smirked*, put the kickstand down on his bike and strode up to our table. "No, siree, they don't have painted rocks or popcorn or a dancing chicken."

He plunked* a fistful of coins down on the stand, which rolled in every direction and into the grass. "Popcorn sounds good. I'll have some. And a lemonade, too. But no rocks.

They're too crunchy for me." He laughed like crazy.

I had to ask. "How do you know what the Tuckers have?"

"I was just there," Sawyer said, trying to stop laughing. "They're selling chips and painted seashells. One of them is dancing around dressed up like a gingerbread man."

I asked him if he'd seen our lucky bell there.

"That doesn't *ring a bell**!" he said, laughing goofily again. Then he admitted he couldn't remember.

For a free lemonade and cupcake, he agreed to bike back over to the Tuckers' stand and take a look around.

"No bell," he reported when he returned.

Was Mr. Hissanfuss the thief after all? Or had Captain Cabot regretted giving up his prized bell and "borrowed" it for a while?

🖤 🖤

There was no use sitting there all day watching the ice melt. The Tuckers were snatching the lemonade business away from us.

Clearly, the lemonade war was over. The Dooleys had to admit that the Tuckers were the winners. We made better lemonade, but they had a better spot for a business since they were right across from the sports field.

The Dooleys weren't giving up on the school fund, though. We had some good ideas on how to raise money, such as holding a car wash, selling friendship bracelets and weeding gardens.

My mom walked with me to the corner market to return the rest of the lemons.

It was a nice surprise to see Anny and her older brother there picking up groceries for dinner, as well as Alejandra, who was helping Señora Sanchez stock the candy shelves.

When I asked my mom if we could buy gum for a bubble-blowing contest at my party, Alejandra's eyes lit up.

"*¡Que divertido!* (How fun!)," Alejandra said.

"That's not all," said Anny. "There will be blimp rides and bungee jumping at Willow's party, too."

My mom gave me the hairy eyeball. That's a look that means I'm in big trouble. It meant that we were going to have "a little chat."

We had that talk on way the home. She understood how things got out of control but it was time to be honest with my friends. "Your birthday party is in just one week. Promise me you will tell the truth. Tomorrow."

During art class the next morning, I was getting up the nerve to keep the promise I'd made to my mom. But before I had a chance, Daisy and I got into a ridiculous* fight. It was about a crayon she was holding. The wrapper with the color name had been torn off.

"That color is called Fire Engine Red," I said.

"No! It's called Candy Apple Red!" Daisy insisted.

"I don't think so," I muttered*.

"Yes it is, Willow!" she squabbled*. "Anybody can see it's the color of a candy apple which, by the way, I will be eating when I go to the Harvest Fair with my friend on Saturday!"

That's the day of my most fantabulous birthday party ever! I realized. *That's why she didn't RSVP*. She had a better offer all along, but didn't want to say so. Until now.*

While I was still steaming mad about that,

Charlie came over and made a pouting face. She had some bad news. She couldn't come to my party. Her family was traveling a few hours away to visit an aunt who was ill.

Was it just an excuse she made up? I wondered. *Had she discovered that there was no chocolate fountain and nothing exciting happening at my party?*

My doubts were interrupted when the principal's voice blared* over the loudspeaker.

"Attention please, students. I have a wonderful announcement. Our school robotics* team has made it to the championships. They will be competing with the guitar-playing spaghetti-eating robot they built!"

There was a lot of whooping. Sadie was on the team and I gave her a high-five.

The principal continued, "Good luck to those students and to their coach, Captain Cabot. We wish you well at the championship this Saturday!"

This Saturday? Now three out of five

friends weren't coming to my party! I was afraid that when Anny and Abrianna found out, they'd cancel, too.

I needed that lucky bell now more than ever. Where in the world was it?

Chapter Nine

RETURN TO SENDER

It was hard to focus on studying that day after school. Too many things were on my mind: not keeping my promise to my mom, not telling the truth to my friends, the missing bell, the failed lemonade stand, and my argument with Daisy.

Any excuse to do something besides homework was fine with me. I filled up one of Puff and Priscilla's bowls with water. I changed the shoelaces on my sneakers from dirty white to green and purple stripes.

When I sat at the kitchen table, Matisse could see my mind was somewhere else. "Why don't you get some fresh air and go see if the mail has been delivered?" she suggested.

Glad for the chance to get outside, I

leaped up, ran to the mailbox and grabbed the bundle of letters that was inside. Flipping through them as I walked up the driveway, I suddenly stopped.

One piece of mail caught my eye. It was a bright green envelope with glittering purple polka dots.

What is my most fantabulous birthday party ever invitation doing in my mailbox? I wondered.

The envelope was addressed to Daisy, but there was a big red stamp across the front that read: "Return To Sender" and "Postage Due." Sure enough, there was no stamp on the invitation. It must have become unstuck and fallen off.

Now I knew why Daisy was upset. She thought that she wasn't invited.

I also understood why Anny, Charlie, Sadie and Abrianna were behaving strangely when they first got the invitation. They thought that I'd left Daisy out.

I called my mom at work to tell her what had happened. She said that just this once, I could do my homework after dinner.

I hopped on my bicycle and Matisse used my mom's. We fastened our helmets and pedaled over to Daisy's house. This was important, and I wanted to straighten things out in person.

I told Daisy that I was sorry that her feelings were hurt. She apologized for reacting the way she did.

If only I'd asked Daisy weeks ago if she was coming to my party, we would have figured the problem out in an instant. I'd been too much of a fraidy cat.

That's the reason I hadn't talked to the Tuckers, too. I had an idea that would allow us both to earn money.

I'd been scared to ask them. *What's the worst that could happen?* I thought. *They'd turn me down.* I had to try.

"Cross your fingers," I said to Matisse as we biked over to Tucker Lane. Matisse agreed to hang back so that I could tackle this on my own.

The Tuckers were kicking a soccer ball around in a yard, but stopped when they saw me ride up the sidewalk.

Taking a deep breath, I told them how much Captain Cabot's bell meant to him and to me. The Tuckers promised that they didn't steal the bell. I believed them.

I explained how the Dooleys' lemonade

stand was raising money to build a school for kids who had none.

Then came the hard part. "Would you consider having your lemonade stand on Saturday only so the Dooleys could have theirs on Sunday?" I asked.

One of the girls said she had her heart set on earning money for a new bike. Another kid said he was saving up for a computer. They could earn the money faster by having their stand all weekend.

They didn't say yes, but they didn't say no. They'd think about it.

Chapter Ten

LET THE PARTY BEGIN

All along I'd been excited that my party was going to take place on the exact day of my birthday.

It was way more important to me to have all my friends at the party, though. We moved the date to the next Saturday so Sadie, Charlie and Daisy could come, too. That was wonderrific (my own made-up word combining wonderful and terrific).

And I finally fessed up about the mix-up with the party plans. None of my friends seemed disappointed. I should have known they would understand.

Plus, my mom agreed that we'd have room for one more person to sleep over. When I invited Alejandra, she said "¡Sí! Me encantaría

(Yes! I'd love to)."

All that homework stuff I thought I'd never need to know? It helped me make a new friend from Peru.

❦ ❦

For the first hour of the party, my friends and I tried our best to speak entirely in Spanish. We didn't want Alejandra to feel left out of our conversation.

But then we got stuck. We were trying to tell her about what our school day was like, and we just couldn't come up with the word for "recess" in Spanish.

I got out my Spanish/English dictionary and started flipping through the pages to find the word.

Alejandra spoke in perfect English. "Okay, I can't torture you like this any longer. The word for recess is *recreo*. And I want to tell you that your Spanish is improving so much."

We all looked at her in surprise.

I was confused. "You speak English?"

She shrugged. "Matisse told me you wanted to practice your Spanish so...."

Sadie threw a pillow at her, which started a hilarious pillow fight.

Afterwards, we got the supplies for "Anny's Salon" out of my dress-up trunk.

I hung up the poster with the hairstyles. We all took turns being "models," sitting in two "salon chairs" (my dining room chairs).

We sprayed our hair lightly with a water bottle, then began combing, brushing and curling.

Anny showed us how to add the finishing touches: butterfly hair extensions, flower headbands and girly heart and flower clips.

My mom took pictures of us in all kinds of glamorous poses. Some were goofy, too.

Then everyone made their own party favor to take home as a reminder of the great time we were having together. We cut colorful flowers and butterflies out of felt and glued them onto barrettes.

We played party games, including a bubble-gum blowing contest. Abrianna blew a bubble inside of a bubble. But Alejandra was the winner, with a bubble the size of a melon! I never laughed so hard in my life.

Later, after everyone sang "Happy Birthday" to me, I made a wish (to find the lucky bell!) and blew out the candles.

We devoured chocolate cake and chocolate ice cream.

The smile on Charlie's face was as wide as the United States!

As I unwrapped my birthday presents, I wrote a list of what everyone gave me. That would jog my memory when I wrote my "thank you" notes:

Fab Birthday Gifts:

1. Flowered rubber boots from Anny (perfect for stomping in puddles on the way to school)

2. Cozy inflatable sleeping bag from Daisy (extra comfy because it's like an air mattress and a sleeping bag, in one!)

3. Adorable, little striped moose handmade by Charlie in her knitting class (soooooooooo cute!)

4. Pretty friendship bracelet made by Abrianna in green and purple (my favorite colors)

5. Framed photo from Sadie (of me snuggling with Priscilla and Puff)

6. Pen Pal* Kit from Alejandra so we can write to each other when she goes home. (Includes a pen with a white kitty on the top, stamps, note cards and envelopes that she's already put her address on)

88

We brought a piece of birthday cake over to Captain Cabot. He was in his backyard flying his latest invention—a remote-controlled mini blimp. Even though it's a miniature* model of a real blimp, it's almost twice as big as I am.

Captain Cabot asked if we'd like to operate the remote control and be the "pilots." It was spectacular to make it move through the air, traveling back and forth between his yard and mine.

"I guess there are blimp rides at your party after all," joked Abrianna.

Before dark, we decided to climb a tree in a small park that's across from my house.

My mom cupped her hands around her mouth and hollered, "Not too high, girls!"

We were halfway up when we found quite a surprise. Resting between two tree branches was a zebra-striped backpack. And right on top of that was a pair of binoculars weighing down an empty purple cupcake wrapper.

"The Tuckers *were* spying on us!" I exclaimed. "They could see everything the Dooleys have been doing from up in this tree."

Peering through the binoculars, I saw something unusual. Five of the Tuckers were creeping up the sidewalk to my front door. They were glancing around to make sure nobody was watching.

"Those sneaky Tuckers," I hissed.

"What's going on?" "What's happening?" my friends asked.

I reported the events as I saw them happen.

"The Tuckers just put two big boxes on my doorstep. The boxes look like presents. They're pushing the doorbell. They're running away!

"Maybe they're returning the lucky bell," I said hopefully, already scrambling down the tree.

One of the boxes was about the weight of the bell. Together we ripped off the wrapping paper. A small note, handwritten in pencil, was stuck sideways in a dozen lemons. It read:

90

> **If life hands you lemons, make lemonade.**

"Great advice, but no bell," I commented.

"The second box feels about the same weight as the first one," remarked Sadie. "There'd better not be more lemons in here."

Fourteen hands tore off the paper.

We were in for the second shocker of the

day. Inside was a smaller box filled with a whole bunch of coins and cash!

We gasped when we read the note inside:

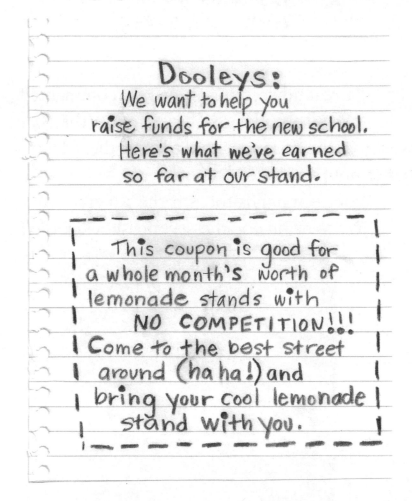

Dooleys:
We want to help you
raise funds for the new school.
Here's what we've earned
so far at our stand.

This coupon is good for
a whole month's worth of
lemonade stands with
NO COMPETITION!!!
Come to the best street
around (ha ha!) and
bring your cool lemonade
stand with you.

Chapter Eleven

THE BURIED TREASURE

Later that night, my friends and I played flashlight tag in the backyard and looked at the moon through my dad's telescope.

Then the pajama party began. I wore my favorite pajamas, the ones with the songbird on the front, and my bunny slippers. We popped popcorn, jumped on the bed and spread out our sleeping bags, which covered my entire bedroom floor.

When my mom said it was time to turn the lights out, Anny told us a scary ghost story she heard at summer camp. We told jokes, and even repeated some of Sawyer's. We whispered and giggled until, one by one, my friends fell asleep.

My eyelids kept drooping shut, but I didn't want the fantabulous night to end.

The last thing I heard before drifting off to sleep was Puff and Priscilla purring, curled up between the sleeping bags.

॰ঌ ঌ॰

The mystery of the missing bell continued until a few days later when Captain Cabot decided to weed his garden.

I'd gone over to thank him for letting my party guests fly his blimp. As we chatted, he sunk his shovel into the earth and it hit something hard. He tried again and the metal made another loud thud*.

He kneeled down and scooped dirt out of the hole he'd been digging. "Well, whaddya know?"

We both stared in amazement. There was the lucky bell!

"Rfff!" Pirate wagged his tail with pride at what he'd "planted" in the garden.

It was impossible not to hug a robber who's so doggone cute.

Chapter Twelve

A GOOD SIGN

The following Saturday, the Dooleys marched over to Tucker Lane with our coupon.

Captain Cabot helped my mom unload the lemonade stand from the back of her pink four-wheel drive vehicle.

It was going to be a busy weekend. There was a big soccer tournament taking place at the Tucker Sports Field. There would also be the usual softball and basketball games, as well as kids and parents going to the playground.

The Tuckers helped us set up our stand right next to theirs so we could spread out all of the things we had for sale: lemonade (in pink and yellow), homemade strawberry and chocolate cupcakes (made by Haley and Jenny), bananas and apples (donated by

Señora Sanchez), friendship bracelets (made by Abrianna) and three little striped moose just like mine (knit by Charlie).

Matisse had given us something to sell, too: Lunch Box Riddle Club membership cards. New members would receive one lunch box math riddle every week for a year.

The Tuckers and Dooleys worked together to hang signs, squeeze lemons and scoop ice.

There were a few helpers who weren't Dooleys or Tuckers. Alejandra was helping pour

lemonade. It was her first lemonade stand ever. Anny was braiding hair at a table off to the side.

100% (every single penny) of the profits* would be donated to Free The Children to help build a school.

Our first customer was Mr. Hissanfuss, who was pushing his baby in her stroller. He said the lemonade was so delicious he'd buy another cup.

Some of the athletes began leaving the field and spotted our stand right away. You couldn't miss the enormous chicken and gingerbread man dancing to music from our flute and tuba players.

I stopped for a second and took in the most fantabulous sight ever.

Friends helping friends. Kids making a difference.

It looked like the lucky bell had worked its magic again. ☺

this is **our** story

We are an extraordinary generation of girls. And have we got a story to tell.

Our Generation is unlike any that has come before. We're helping our families learn to recycle, holding bake sales to support charities, even holding penny drives to build homes for orphaned children in Haiti. We're helping our little sisters learn to read and even making sure the new kid at school has a place to sit in the cafeteria.

All that and we still find time to play hopscotch and hockey. To climb trees, do cartwheels all the way down the block and laugh with our friends until milk comes out of our noses. You know, to be kids.

Will we have a big impact on the world? We already have. What's ahead for us? What's ahead for the world? We have no idea. We're too busy grabbing and holding on to the joy that is today.

Yep. This is our time. This is our story.

www.ogdolls.com

Glossary

*Many words have more than one meaning. Here are the definitions of words marked with this symbol * (an asterisk) as they are used in sentences.*

anxious: *uneasy and worried*
ASAP: *As Soon As Possible*
awkward: *uncomfortable*
bash: *party*
beans, as in "spilled the beans": *make a secret known without meaning to*
bell, as in "ring a bell": *sound familiar*
besties: *nickname for best friends*
BFFs: *Best Friends Forever*
blared: *made a loud sound*
blue: *sad*
chops: *the area around the mouth*
chuckled: *laughed quietly*
craze: *a thing that's popular*
dorm: *short for dormitory, a building that*

students live in at a college

dread: *fear mixed with worry*

Dutch, as in "double Dutch": *a jump-rope game played with two long ropes that are swung in opposite directions*

embarrassment: *the feeling of being uncomfortable and ashamed*

exaggerate: *to make something seem larger or worse than it really is*

fantabulous: *fantastic and fabulous*

fib: *a lie*

fidgety: *making movements because of being nervous and impatient*

fizzling: *ending in a disappointing way*

frolicking: *playing in a happy way*

fumed: *showed anger*

funds: *money saved for a specific reason*

galore: *in a great amount*

glanced: *looked*

grander: *more magnificent*

hilarious: *very funny*

inflatable: *able to be filled with air*

mammoth: *huge*

miniature: *a very small copy of something*

mumbled: *said quietly and not clearly*

musty: *stale, moldy*

muttered: *spoke in a low voice or grumbled*

off the wall: *unusual and perhaps a little weird*

over the top: *above or beyond what is normal or expected*

pal, as in "Pen Pal": *a friend you keep in touch with by writing letters*

plunked: *put down or dropped suddenly*

profits: *the amount of money left after subtracting the amount it cost to make something*

ridiculous: *silly, foolish*

robotics: *having to do with creating robots*

RSVP: *let someone who is giving a party know if you will or will not be able to go*

scowled: *looked irritated*

shrill: *high-pitched, piercing*

smirked: *smiled in a silly way*

sprawled: *to sit with arms and legs spread out in a relaxed way*

squabbled: *argued noisily*
struck, as in "struck up": *began*
sulking: *showing a bad mood*
tarnished: *dull and stained*
tart: *sour in taste*
thud: *heavy, dull sound*
tinkering: *repairing or improving things*
tweaks: *small changes*
vocabulary: *words of a language*
waggled: *moved back and forth in quick, short movements*

Lunch Box Riddle Club Fun

Matisse turns lunchtime into a fun time with math tricks and brainteasers. Make copies of these pages, cut on the dotted lines and stash one of these surprises along with your sandwich. Do you buy your lunch at school? Tuck one in your pocket to take with you.

Calculator Magic

Find the answer to this riddle with a simple calculator.
(Clue: It's one of Captain Cabot's favorite tools.)

1. Enter the number of days in a year.
2. Divide that by the number of toes on your right foot.
3. Press the equal sign.
4. Add the number of candles on Willow's birthday cake.
5. Press the equal sign.
6. Multiply that by the number of Priscilla's paws.
7. Press the equal sign.
8. Subtract the total number of days there are in the month of February (when it's not a leap year).
9. Press the equal sign.
10. Turn your calculator upside down to see the answer spelled out!

Pound Puzzler

You are at the cash register at the corner market.
Señora Sanchez, the owner of the store, puts your purchases into two bags.

The red bag contains a pound of lemons.
The blue bag contains a pound of pink cotton candy.

Which bag weighs more?

104

Comical Cobs

Captain Cabot loves to garden. This year he's grown more corn than he can eat. He puts a sign in his yard that says:

Pick Your Own Corn
It's tasty, fresh and free!
C'mon in and help yourself.

When you walk into his garden, you count 22 ears of corn. When you walk out of the garden you have 3 ears.

How much corn is still in Captain Cabot's garden?

Number Fun

In math class, your teacher writes this on the chalkboard:
IX=9
She explains that the Roman numeral IX
(as used in ancient Rome) has a value of 9.

Your homework assignment is to make IX into a 6
by adding just one line—
without lifting your pencil o☐ the paper.

How will you do this?
(Your teacher gives you a hint: This answer is more about being creative than about math.)

*Answers are on the About the Author page. No peeking yet! ☺

Power of a Girl Initiative

For every Our Generation doll, outfit or accessory you buy, 10¢ goes to Free The Children's Power of a Girl Initiative to help provide girls in developing countries an education—the most powerful tool in the world for escaping poverty.

Did you know that out of the millions of children who aren't in school, 70% of them are girls? In developing communities around the world, many girls can't go to school. Usually it's because there's no school available or because their responsibilities to family (farming, earning an income, walking hours each day for water) prevent it.

Free The Children has now built more than 650 schools which educate more than 50,000 children throughout the developing world. Free The Children also builds and fosters sustainable villages through healthcare, water programs and alternate income projects for moms and dads that give girls the opportunity to get the education they need.

The most incredible part is that most of Free The Children's funding comes from kids just like you, holding lemonade stands, bake sales, penny drives, walkathons and more.

Just by buying an Our Generation doll or accessory you have helped change the world, and you are powerful (beyond belief!) to help even more.

If you want to find out more, visit:
www.freethechildren.com/girls

FREE THE CHILDREN
children helping children through education

Free The Children provided the factual information pertaining to their organization.
Free The Children is a 501c3 organization.

About the Author

Susan Cappadonia Love lives in Milton, Massachusetts with her husband, Scott and daughters, Sophie and Olivia.

*In addition to **The Most Fantabulous Pajama Party Ever**, she has also written six other books in the Our Generation® Series, **The Jukebox Babysitters**, **The Dress in the Window**, **The Sweet Shoppe Mystery**, **The Mystery of the Vanishing Coin**, **Stars in Your Eyes** and **One Smart Cookie**, as well as other children's books.*

Many, many thanks to Gisela Voss, Lisa Carmack, Sue DeFalco, Kate Annantuonio and Pam Shrimpton. Much gratitude goes to all the wonderful people at Maison Joseph Battat Ltd., including Joe Battat, Dany Battat, Alison Morin, Batia Tarrab, Natalie Cohen, Loredana Ramacieri, Karen Erlichman and Lisa Skolnick.

Lunch Box Riddle Club Answers

Calculator Magic: 304 (upside down it spells "hoe").

Pound Puzzler: Both bags are the same weight—one pound.

Comical Cobs: The answer is that there are two answers! The answer is 19 if you are subtracting 3 from 22. Or, the answer is 21 if you picked 1 ear and add your own 2 ears (the ones on your head).

Number Fun: Add a curvy line in the shape of an "S" in front of IX and—drum roll, please—you get SIX!

Calculator Fun on Page 35: 53045 (shoes)